SISTER

Tell Me Your Life Story

This Book is For:

_____

_____

Date: _____

What would you change, if anything, about our experience growing up?

Date:

What do you admire most about Mom and/or Dad?

Date:_____

In what ways did Mom or Dad let you down?

Date: _ _ _ _ _ _ _ _ _ _ _ _

What's something you wish you could
have told me when we were kids? Why
didn't you tell me then?

Date:_____

How could I have been a better sibling to you when we were growing up?

Date: _____

What's your favorite childhood memory of us?

Date: _____

What's the worst fight we've ever had?

Date: _____

Who was the first person to break your heart?

Date:

Were you ever bullied? Did you ever bully anyone?

Date:_____

What's my most annoying habit or quality?

Date:_____

What memory of us still makes you laugh?

Date:_____

Do you think our parents had a favorite kid? If so, who and why?

Date:_____

What was your biggest insecurity as a teenager?

Date:_____

How did you lose your virginity?

Date:_____

What's your love language?

Date: _____

If you had a Saturday with no plans, how would you spend it?

Date: _____

What event in your life has had the most significant impact on you?

Date:_____

What is your biggest worry these days and why?

Date:_____

Where's a place you wish you could live for a few months?

Date:_____

Do you consider yourself successful?

Date:_____

What's your hidden talent?

Date:_____

What would you change, if anything, about our experience growing up?

Date:-------------

What's one healthy thing you do to manage stress? And one unhealthy thing?

Date:_____

Do you believe in God or a higher power?

Date:_____

What's something you wish more people knew about you?

Date:_____

What's the social or political cause you're most passionate about?

Date:_____

Who would you want to give the eulogy at your funeral?

Date: _____

What's a mean comment someone made about you that's stuck with you to this day?

Date:_____

What's the most rebellious thing you've ever done?

Date:_____

When do you feel the most confident?

Date: _____

If salary and experience didn't matter, what job would you most want to have?

Date:_____

What song or movie scene makes you cry without fail?

Date:_____

If we could go on a dream trip together, where would we go and what would we do there?

Date:_____

How do you feel about getting older?

Date:_____

What's something that scares you now that you hope you do before you die?

Date:_____

How would you describe your relationship with money?

PHOTOGRAPHS & MEMORABILIA

PHOTOGRAPHS & MEMORABILIA

Date:_____

What's been the best day of your life so far?

Date:_____

How many kids do you really want to have?

Date:_____

When, where and who was your first kiss?

Date:_____

If you could meet anyone in the world, alive or dead, who would it be?

Date:_____

What's been the best day of your life so far?

Date:_____

How did you really feel about the last gift I bought you?

Date:_____

What was a moment in college or high school that you'd never want to relive?

Date:_____

Who would play you in a movie? Okay, now who *should* play you in a movie?

Date:_____

If you could go back in time, would you change what you wore to prom?

Date:_____

Is there something I did that you've never gotten over, or forgiven?

Date:_____

On a scale from one to 10 how
uncomfortable are you answering these
questions?

Date:_____

When did you tell mom and dad that you
started drinking? When did
you *actually* have your first drink?

Date:_____

Which of our siblings is actually your favorite?

Date:_____

What's one piece of parental advice that you've held onto?

Date:

What is your guilty TV pleasure?

Date: _____

Have you ever had a night you couldn't remember? If so what led up to it?

Date: _____

What's your greatest fear in life?

Date:_____

Which sibling loves reading books more?

Date:_____

Does your sibling love sweets? Which are their favorites?

Date: _____

Which one of you is more spoiled?

Date:_____

Do you plan to study or have you already studied at the same university?

Date: _____

What is the one thing that has changed the most about your sibling as he/she has become older?

Date:_____

What's your sibling's favorite song and what song is their guilty pleasure?

Date:

Which one of you is more creative?

Date:_____

Which one of you is able to sing better?

Date:_____

Who has better dance moves?

Date:_____

Who is more pessimistic/optimistic?

Date:

Who is more introverted/extroverted?

Date:_____

Complete this statement:
My brother/sister is really bad at...?

Date:

Which one of you is able to sing better?

Date:_____

Do you remember your biggest fight? What was it about?

Date:_____

Does your sibling have a favorite animal?

Date:_____

Do you like to go shopping together?

Date:

Who is your sibling's favorite celebrity?

Date:_____

Who is a better driver and who is a danger on the road?

Date:_____

What is your sibling's biggest regret?

Date:_____

What are the qualities and the personality traits your sibling appreciates the most in others?

Date:_____

What are your sibling's three most common habits?

Date:_____

Did your sibling ever help you get out of trouble?

Date:_____

Who is better at party planning?

Date: _____

Who is the person, dead or alive, imaginary or real, your sibling would like to share a meal and a conversation with the most?

Date:_____

Did you ever hide something from your sibling?

PHOTOGRAPHS & MEMORABILIA

PHOTOGRAPHS & MEMORABILIA

Date:

Date:

Date:

Date:

Date:

Date:

Date:

Date:

Date:

Date:

Date:

Date:

Date:

Date:

Date:

Date:

Made in the USA
Coppell, TX
20 December 2024

43056078R00057